SINGAPORE·CHILDREN'S·FAVOURITE·STORIES

SINGAPORE CHILDREN'S FAVOURITE STORIES

TEXT BY
DI TAYLOR

ILLUSTRATIONS BY
L K TAY-AUDOUARD

PERIPLUS

For my parents, who first introduced me to the charms of Singapore when I was six months old. — Di Taylor
For Father, with whom all things are possible. And for the child in all of us. — L.K. Tay-Audouard

Published by Periplus Editions (HK) Ltd.

www.periplus.com

Text © 2003 Diane Kay Taylor
Illustrations © 2003 Lak-Khee Tay-Audouard
All rights reserved. No part of this publication
may be reproduced, stored in a retrieval system,
or transmitted, in any form or by any means,
electronic, mechanical, photocopying, recording
or otherwise, without the prior written permission
of the publisher.

ISBN 978-0-7946-0097-6
First printing 2003

Distributed by

Asia Pacific: Berkeley Books Pte Ltd,
61 Tai Seng Avenue, #02-12, Singapore 534167
tel: (65) 6280 3320; fax: (65) 6280 6290
email: inquiries@periplus.com.sg
www.periplus.com

Indonesia: PT Java Books Indonesia
Kawasan Industri Pulogadung
Jl. Rawa Gelam IV No. 9, Jakarta 13930
tel: (62) 21 4682-1088; fax: (62) 20 461-0206
email: crm@periplus.co.id
www.periplus.com

Japan: Tuttle Publishing
Yaekari Building, 3rd Floor
5-4-12 Osaki, Shinagawa-ku, Tokyo 141-0032
Tel: (81) 3 5437-0171; Fax: (81) 3 5437-0755
email: sales@tuttle.co.jp; www.tuttle.co.jp

North America, Latin America & Europe:
Tuttle Publishing, 364 Innovation Drive,
North Clarendon, VT 05759-9436 USA.
tel: 1 (802) 773 8930; fax: 1 (802) 773 6993
email: info@tuttlepublishing.com
www.tuttlepublishing.com

Printed in China   1605RR
19 18 17 16   12 11 10 9 8

CONTENTS

HOW THE ISLAND OF SINGAPORE CAME ABOUT

There once lived a terrible, cruel King called Hai Loong Wang. He ruled his kingdom by bullying, and his people were all terrified of him. His kingdom was made up of volcanic cones buried deep under the ocean, so deep that no human dreamt such a place could exist. Shilepo was the name of the largest of these cones.

The people of Shilepo were mermaids and mermen, who lived happily together in their underwater paradise. The flowers in their gardens were colourful corals whose fronds and tentacles twisted and floated in the warm water currents in their search for food. Their trees were the mighty seaweeds that grew hundreds of feet up from the sea-bed. It was said that the tops of these magnificent trees were gathered and used as food by strange, two-legged land creatures.

As for the mer-people, they planted sea cucumbers, anemones and other rock treasures for their food. Their pets were sea horses, urchins and turtles. Their playground was the ocean bed itself.

Now Hai Loong Wang had many rules. The main rule was posted on signs all around the kingdom.

BY ORDER OF THE KING !
SWIMMING·OUTSIDE·THE·MER·KINGDOM
IS·STRICTLY·FORBIDDEN
RULE·BREAKERS·WILL·BE·BANISHED

Actually, none of the mer-people wanted to leave their magical home. Most of them never even dared to dream about a different life above the sea.

All except one mermaid, that is. Her name was Sea Plum, and she was the brightest mermaid in all Shilepo. Her cleverness often got her into trouble, as she was inquisitive, bold and sharp-witted. She was always restless, and wanted to have real adventures.

Bored with playing hide-and-seek with her friends, she frequently dreamt about a life outside. The more she thought about it, the more she was convinced that there must be other places to go. To Sea Plum, the invisible boundaries felt like prison bars.

One day, while she was playing with her big sister Sea Pearl, she decided to run away. Because she was scared, Sea Plum decided to confide in Sea Pearl.

"You know we're told that we can't swim far up the river or sea monsters will eat us, and that will be the end of us?" asked Sea Plum.

"Yes, we all know that," replied Sea Pearl.

"Well, I don't believe that anymore," retorted Sea Plum. "I've seen the King coming back from up-river many times. Sometimes he brings treasures. Last week, I saw him towing a whole ship back, and once he carried a creature with no tail but two legs. He collects gems, gold, jewellery and other precious things from the ships that sail above us. I'm sure of it."

"Questioning the King's rules will only bring us trouble," replied Sea Pearl, as she nervously looked around to see if anyone else was listening. "Anyway, what's so awful about staying here?"

"Oh don't be so boring," scorned Sea Plum. "Come with me. We'll swim up-river while we have the chance. We could go right now and be back in time for lunch."

"We can't go against his orders," said Sea Pearl meekly, "even if the King is lying and we find all kinds of things, we would be in serious trouble with everyone else. "

"I don't care," declared Sea Plum. "I'm going with or without you. I just need to know one way or another what lies outside our kingdom."

With that Sea Plum swam defiantly up-current, leaving Sea Pearl perched on a rock, being a sensible big sister, and wondering what she should do next.

Sea Pearl waited for what seemed like hours, getting more and more worried about Sea Plum's safety. Had she been eaten by sea monsters?

Would she be kidnapped by passing ships? Had she been swallowed up by a storm? She dared not go home, because of course everyone would ask where Sea Plum was. She began plucking uneasily at her scales, counting them to pass the time as she waited.

Suddenly she saw Sea Plum, swimming towards her, glowing with happiness. She grabbed her sister by the hand and breathlessly told her what she had seen.

"I did it! I really did it, Sea Pearl! I went right to the top of the ocean, and I found myself in another world. There are no sea monsters or anything to stop us — the King has lied to us all this time so he can keep his secrets. What a greedy man! Come ON, Sea Pearl. Come and see things that will make your eyes wobble."

She stopped to pause for breath, her green eyes shining brightly amidst the tangle of her flowing mermaid hair. In the midst of the tangles, Sea Pearl spotted something shimmering and glinting.

"What's that?" she asked. "You've got something stuck in your hair."

"It's a gift, a present. Look!" chattered Sea Plum. From beneath the tangles she pulled out a beautiful hair comb, studded with glittering gems. "The creatures on the ships threw all kinds of things to me, that's why I came to get you. Come ON! Have some fun for a change."

By the next day, Sea Plum had managed to persuade Sea Pearl to join her on her next adventure. Together the two mermaids swam away from their home. Sea Plum led the way, gliding confidently through the water in full command. Sea Pearl, still unsure, followed more slowly, stopping every now and then to glance behind nervously.

They soon reached the top of the ocean, where a rainbow arced across the clear blue sky. Large sea birds flew close to them, and the girls rolled, splashed and dived happily into the waves. Sea Pearl soon forgot her worries. In the distance they saw ships of all kinds, and as one of the ships grew closer, they could see strange two-legged creatures aboard.

11

"Come on, let's swim really close," called Sea Plum over the crests of the waves. "I did it before — they threw presents to me last time!" she giggled.

But Sea Pearl was still nervous and shook her head. As her sister swam off, Sea Pearl wondered what to do. Should she turn back? Or should she follow her younger sister? She had a strange feeling that something dreadful would happen at any moment.

She struck out through the waves after her sister, sure now that they must get home as soon as possible. As she drew near to the ship she heard the strange creatures calling out, and yes! . . . even throwing things into the water for them to catch. Sea Plum was laughing and splashing her tail as she dived for the treasures like a performing dolphin.

"Sea Plum! Stop! We've got to go . . . " Sea Pearl began. But as she called out to her sister she sensed danger. The weather had suddenly changed. The waves grew higher and rougher, the wind blew and the air filled with the cracking of thunder. Flashes of lightning ripped the sky apart. The ship began to toss around like a cork in a bath-tub.

"What is it?" cried Sea Plum. She, too, was frightened now.

"I think it's the King. Can you feel the water sucking everything down? I think he's come for that ship, and if we don't move fast he'll catch us up here. Swim for your life, Sea Plum. SWIM!"

The two girls disappeared back under the waves, and tried as hard as they could to swim back to the sea-bed, but try as they might, they found they couldn't. Something was holding them back. All of a sudden, out of the churning water ahead of them appeared a menacing figure. It was the King!

"STAY WHERE YOU ARE!" he bellowed. "How dare you disobey the orders of the kingdom. You know what the punishment is, don't you?"

The two mermaids stared at him, trembling from head to tail, praying that he would be kind and let them go home.

But he didn't.

"From this moment on you will be turned into mud-skippers," he roared. "For ten thousand years you and your people will only be able to crawl on your bellies, and slither helplessly in and out of the water's edge. Perhaps then you will learn to obey the orders of your King." The King waved his golden staff through the waters around them and . . .

BOOM! . . .

The whole underwater cone of Shilepo shook and trembled and began to rise up through the water. The sea swirled angrily around it, foaming and crashing onto its edges, and as the cone rose the two mermaids felt themselves shrinking smaller and smaller.

Suddenly everything fell silent. The top half of the cone was by now an island basking in the heat of the tropical sun, its shores awash by a calm sea. The King was nowhere to be seen. Sea Plum and Sea Pearl looked around them in bewilderment.

They were lying on the ground. All around them were slimy, wriggling creatures, sliding into the sea on their bellies, and trying to climb out again. The mermaids realized that not only they, but all the other mer-people of the kingdom, had been outcast by the king and transformed into mud-skippers. They were terribly ashamed, but it was too late to be sorry now. Their recklessness had brought disaster not only on themselves, but on the whole mer-community.

However, all was not lost. The mud-skippers eventually learnt to live in their new home and soon Shilepo became a thriving island. Fisher-people moved there. Traders. Merchants. People came from all over to settle on this beautiful island, but no-one suspected the true story of how it had come about.

So, next time you see a mud-skipper, be kind to it. Remind yourself that you might be looking at Sea Pearl or Sea Plum, the adventurous mermaids, who along with their families and friends are still waiting to return to their own beautiful kingdom beneath the waves.

T H E · L A S T · T I G E R

ong ago, on the island of Singapore, there were huge tracts of jungle, ancient trees and lots of wild animals. Tigers roamed the land quite freely. In those days, people hunted and killed the tigers, and soon there were none left.

At this time, gambier trees were grown in huge forests called plantations. One of the largest gambier plantations was by a village named Choa Chu Kang, in the north of Singapore. Hundreds of workers came to the plantations, to work planting new trees, or chopping down the old ones to be sold. Some collected gambier leaves to make dye. Sometimes the workers laboured in pairs or groups, but often they worked alone.

16

It was a very lonely job. In the evenings, the workers swapped stories. One evening, as they sat round chatting, one worker mentioned, "I heard there is a tiger around. It stole a goat from Choa Chu Kang village yesterday."

"Don't be silly — there can't be," said another, "there are no tigers left in Singapore. I heard from the villagers that a man named Peng Hoe has helped to track down and kill them all."

"Still, if it is true," said the first, "we'll have to be careful. An old and hungry tiger will be desperate enough to eat anything. We've got nothing to defend ourselves with."

Each plantation had a head man, or *kangchu*, and this one was named Wang. He was a busy and rather impatient man, full of self-importance. On this particular day he was also very worried, because he had heard some bad news. Two of his workers had been killed and eaten by a wild and hungry tiger during the week. It seemed that the tiger had stealthily crept up on each of them while they were working, pounced, and made a meal of them before they could even shout for help. The only thing the tiger left behind was their rather chewy leather hats.

Wang was not only worried for his workers, he was also worried for his own safety, and had no intention of having his life threatened by a tiger. He called a meeting of all the plantation workers.

"I'm sure you have heard that we have lost two men this week to a roaming tiger. No-one has seen him and lived to tell the tale, but his hungry roar has been heard many times. There will be a $10 reward for the person who can kill this animal, before he takes any more of our men."

One plantation worker raised his hand: "Sir, we all want to catch him for we're afraid out there in the plantation alone, but we have no weapons apart from our *parangs*. Can you supply us with guns?"

Now the only gun for miles around belonged to Wang himself, and he was too afraid to even think about trying to shoot the tiger himself, so he kept this information quiet. He would rather risk his men than put his own life in danger.

"There are no guns here," he lied. "Anyway, are you such cowards that you can't face an old tiger with a *parang*? You are young. You are well fed. You are fit. This tiger is old. The reward will now be $20 for the man who gets rid of this tiger!"

And with that, he left the meeting.

The next day, two workers came to his office, heads bowed, gripping their hats in their shaking hands. "Master Wang, the tiger has struck again," one of them said, nervously. "This time we saw it happen. It was terrible. He leapt out from behind a tree and seized worker Li. Before any of us could get near, it had already dragged him into the trees. It all happened very fast and we can't find any sign of poor Li. There's just nothing left of him."

Wang was afraid. "Next time you see that tiger, don't just stand there — kill it!"

The two workers left his office, by now very angry with Wang.

"It's all very well for him to give us orders, but his servant told me that he owns the only gun in the village. He should stalk and shoot the tiger himself!"

"He's a coward," replied his friend. "He would rather we risked our own lives."

That evening, after work, the two men called some of the plantation workers together to form a plan.

"Men, this is a dangerous time for us. We must find that tiger and kill it before it gets any more of us," said one.

"But everyone knows that tigers are faster and stronger than humans," called out another worker. "They run fast, they climb trees, they can even swim — we don't stand a chance. We only have our small *parangs*. They are no match against a tiger's teeth and claws."

A young man stepped forward. He was from the local village of Choa Chu Kang.

"I can help you," he said. "My name is Peng Hoe, and I have helped the villagers of Choa Chu Kang hunt down the other tigers. I heard that Master Wang owns a gun. If this is true, I will ask if I can borrow it and I will track down the tiger myself."

The men were so relieved at his offer of help that immediately they took Peng Hoe to meet Master Wang.

"You're right," replied Wang, when asked, "I do own a gun and I am happy to lend it to you. I will give you bullets and $20 if you kill the tiger."

With that he placed a large rifle into Peng Hoe's hands and wished him the very best of luck.

Peng Hoe went back to the waiting workers and showed them the gun.

"I can do this alone," he said, "Or you can help me. If I do it alone, it may take some time. If I have 20 men to help me track down the tiger we can finish the job tonight. Once we know where it is, I will kill it with a single shot. We must not lose any more men to this animal. If I am killed, take the gun back to Wang. At least we will have tried."

The crowd clapped and cheered Peng Hoe, and many volunteered to help him. He selected twenty men and asked them to assemble at dusk.

That night, dressed in dark clothing, each of these men carrying an empty tin can and a stick, arrived at the agreed starting point for the tiger hunt. They followed their instructions faithfully. They fanned out, making a long line through the plantation, shouting and banging the tin cans with their sticks as loudly as they could to scare the tiger out of its hiding place.

Under the cover of the trees, the nervous men moved slowly forwards. It was hard to see in the dim light, and the shadows played tricks on them many times. Then suddenly there came a terrific roar as a huge tiger leapt out right in front of them. Confused and angered by the noise, and faced with so many humans, it was unsure on which one to pounce.

Peng Hoe's plan was working! Although terrified, the men carried on banging their tin cans as they closed ranks around the tiger.

Now it was trapped in this circle of men, snarling and showing its teeth. Calmly Peng Hoe stepped forward, aimed his rifle carefully, and . . .

BANG! . . .

He shot the tiger stone dead. The beautiful but deadly creature lay at the feet of twenty-one men, and for a split second no-one moved.

Then Peng Hoe lowered his rifle, and approached the tiger warily. Standing in front of it, he touched the tiger to make sure it really was dead. When they saw him nod his head, the men went wild. They lifted Peng Hoe into the air and carried him all the way back to Wang's house, singing at the tops of their voices, to tell him the great news.

Wang shook Peng Hoe's hand and gratefully paid him the $20 reward. Thank goodness, he didn't have to worry about losing any more men.

And as for Peng Hoe, he became a hero, and has been remembered ever since as the man who killed the last wild tiger in Singapore.

Surrounding the tropical island of Singapore is, of course, water. On bright sunny days the ocean glows blue like the most luminous of sapphires. On stormy days it turns grey, with angry white caps on the tips of the waves.

One stormy day, when the sea was lashing angrily at the coast-line sweeping in piles of weed and driftwood and flinging them onto the shore, a shoal of wild swordfish swept in with the tide. These creatures were fierce, with sword-like snouts that were as sharp as bread knives. They crunched into anything that happened to be in their path. They snapped and chopped and chomped and chewed.

Some fishermen were standing on the rocks, hoping for a catch. Just one of these huge swordfish would feed a whole family for a week. But they were not so lucky. The fierce fish swept in so quickly, that soon not one fisherman was left. They were all knocked into the water, or eaten, or both.

Some villagers nearby saw what was happening and were terrified. One or two went near to the water to take a closer look and — quick as a flash — were also seized by the swordfish. No-one else dared go near after that. The shaken villagers didn't know what to do next.

"Aeeiiyah!" one cried. "It's a curse!"

"The Gods of the Sea are angry with us," cried another.

"It's the Raja's enemies," said yet another.

"I'll go straight to the Raja and tell him," said a quick-thinking man, whose name was Ong. "He'll know what to do."

And off he ran to the Raja's palace, which was about a half an hour away for a fast runner.

The ruler of Singapore at this time was called Raja Iskander. He was a fearsome man. He was tall like a giant, with a mane of wiry black hair. As bold as he was bossy. As cold as he was cruel. As mad as he was mean. Ong reached the palace and panted his message to the guards on the palace gate.

Now the Raja was curious about these swordfish. This wasn't the kind of problem you hear about every day.

"Come through, come through!" commanded the Raja, "I want to hear more about this."

Ong told the Raja all that he and the other villagers had seen. The Raja decided to take a look for himself. Perhaps one of his enemies had sent the fish as a trap, or as a warning. He ordered fifty of his men to escort him to the beach.

When they arrived at the shore, the soldiers stood at the water's edge. Making sure he did not get too close, the Raja scanned the water. Nothing moved. The sun was high in the sky, and the sea was completely smooth, like sparkling turquoise silk.

He watched as some of the soldiers began to patrol the beach. All was quiet. Just as they stepped into the shallows, there came a colossal . . .

SNAP!

And in the twinkling of an eye they were under attack. Hundreds of snapping jaws leapt out of the greeny-blue water at the same time, creating huge waves. They grabbed at the confused men. In another twinkling the soldiers disappeared under the foamy waves, clasped in the jaws of the vicious fish.

The Raja panicked.

"Destroy the fish!" he commanded, "Use your weapons. Don't let them get away!"

But try as they might, the rest of the soldiers could not even get near. They tried to stab them with spears but faster than lightning, the huge fish lunged out. Thrashing wildly their beaks speared the soldiers instead.

The sea ran red with blood, and as the waves pounded the beach, they washed right up to where the Raja was standing. Raja Iskander, watching all this, was shocked by the awful sight.

He was just wondering what to do next, when a small boy ran boldly up to him.

"Sir, order your soldiers to step back from the water. I spend lots of time fishing round here. I've seen these swordfish before. They stab anything that gets in their way. They will just kill all your soldiers, and come back for more. I have another idea that you should try! How about you get the soldiers to build a kind of trap? That way you can catch all the swordfish easily, and no-one else will get hurt."

The Raja could hardly believe his ears. Here was a small boy, only about seven years old, giving a Raja instructions on what to do. He was actually rather offended that this cheeky boy would have enough courage to even approach him, never mind make a suggestion. But

as he had no better idea himself he decided to let him speak.

"Well young man, if you have an answer to this problem, better let me hear it."

"You must build a wall," said the lad. "Banana stems will do. Build it all along the edge of the sea just here. Then when the fish come back on the next tide, the first thing they will do is attack the stems. Their sword-beaks will get stuck in the wall and they'll be trapped."

"Hmmmmm! It's a simple enough plan," replied the Raja, stroking his beard. "It just might work. What's the harm in trying?"

So the Raja commanded his men to come away from the water, and to collect banana stems instead. The relieved soldiers went quickly in search of banana trees.

By the time the sun set, the tide had gone out, and all the swordfish had vanished with it. Not even one was to be seen.

"They will be back on the next high tide," the boy advised the Raja. "You must build the trap quickly so it's in place by the time they come back."

The soldiers returned, group by group, bringing back bundles of banana stems. Soon great stacks of banana stems were piled along the shore. The soldiers began to build the fence, despite the dark, guided by the little boy. They rammed the stems into the ground all along the edge of the sea. They bound them firmly together. This made a firm fence between the fish and the people.

The next day when the tide came in, again it carried hundreds of the swordfish with it. As the boy had said, they jabbed and stabbed their swords in all directions. Soon their sword-beaks were firmly jammed into the woody stems. Within fifteen minutes, every single swordfish was stuck fast. The soldiers quickly killed the trapped fish and gave them to the villagers for a feast. Soon, there were no more swordfish left in the water.

Now the Raja was troubled by something else. Everyone was so delighted that the plan had worked, that the boy was getting lots of attention.

"Well done, boy!" the villagers congratulated him. "Come and see us any time you like. We're very grateful!"

"Interesting!" thought the Raja to himself, "This child is so clever that he can rid the island of deadly swordfish with just one simple idea. He has become popular too. He might grow up to be very powerful. He could take my position. I can't take that risk — I will have to do something about him, and do it fast."

By the end of the morning the Raja had decided what to do. He would have the boy secretly killed. But by this time, the boy could not be found.

"That boy, the one who told us to build the fence," said the Raja to one of the villagers. "Where does he live?"

"He lives with his grandmother, in the smallest wooden hut on top of that hill," replied the villager, pointing to the forested hill behind them.

"Captain!" the Raja called to one of his soldiers. "Find that boy and kill him immediately." He added in a low voice: "He is dangerous."

"Yes, Sir!" the captain saluted. Right or wrong, no-one dared to question the Raja.

The Captain took two soldiers with him. Hacking through the undergrowth and pushing aside branches that hung down like snakes, they wound their way up the over-grown path that led from the beach. In a clearing they found the tiny wooden hut. The boy wasn't at home, but a strange old woman with long white hair was there. Her face was as craggy as a walnut, and her nose almost touched her curiously curved chin.

Before the Captain had even opened his mouth to ask for the boy, she spoke. "I know why you are here," she quavered, pointing a long bony finger at them. "You should be here to reward the boy who saved the lives of the army, and the fishermen. But your Raja is wicked. He wants you to kill the very child who helped you. I will teach you a lesson." Her voice rose to a shriek, "I'll punish you all!"

The terrified soldiers fled back down the path, away from this witch. As they struggled and tripped through the forest, they heard her cackling and singing.

"Run, run! You can't escape me!" They tried to run faster, but found that they were hardly moving at all. Some kind of magical power was holding them back. Suddenly, a hole opened in the ground in front of them, and thick, red liquid began to ooze from the ground. Faster it came, bubbling and fizzing by now, pouring down the hill, and turning all the soil red.

"Until the small boy returns, this hill will remain the colour of blood," they could hear the old woman screeching. "This is a message to the island people to tell them of their cruel Raja and how he has made a big mistake."

The plague of swordfish never returned, and the old woman and small boy have not been seen again.

In fact, you might actually have been to the place where this happened. It is called Red Hill, or Bukit Merah, and the soil there is still red to this day.

QUEEN·OF·THE·FOREST

Long ago there lived a beautiful Malay princess whose name was Ria. Sadly, her mother had died while Ria was still a baby, but her father, whose name was King Aman, worshipped his lovely little daughter. Ria's hair was gleaming black, and flowed right down her back. She usually wore a red ribbon in it. Her face was open and friendly, and her dark eyes sparkled with fun.

Princess Ria didn't have any brothers or sisters. So King Aman tried to make her life as wonderful as he possibly could. She had lots and lots of servants. She had seven just to cook her favourite dishes each day. Three to make the latest clothes. Two to read her favourite stories to her, and to help her learn to read and write. Another taught her to sing. She even had a servant to bathe her, brush her hair and clean her teeth. She never had to lift a finger to do anything.

You're probably thinking that she must have been a spoilt and horrible little girl. But funnily enough, she wasn't. She was actually very chatty, really friendly, and terribly kind and sweet.

One day, when she was sixteen years old, the King thought it was time for her to get married. Girls got married very young in those days, especially princesses. "My dear, I am trying to find you a good husband," he said. "One who will share your life, be fun to talk to, and be as kind as you are."

To tell the truth, Ria did not want to get married. She loved her life at the palace with all her servants. Why would she need anyone else?

The King told everyone he knew that he needed a husband for his daughter, and soon those people told everyone else. Before long, princes were coming to the palace every day. They usually came on horseback, or sometimes in a carriage. One even came on the back of an elephant. They came from nearby, and they came from faraway places that Ria had never heard of. All they could talk about was how important they were, or how much gold they had. She found them all very boring. None of them were any fun, and not one of them seemed sweet or kind. In fact, none of them took any real notice of her.

One evening, King Aman held a huge banquet in the palace garden. Twelve hundred people were invited. Kings and Queens, Princes and Princesses, Sultans and Sultanas. There were mountains of crisp shiny grilled meats, crunchy green vegetables in tasty sauces, exotic rice dishes, swirling, steaming noodles and colourful homemade cakes. Fresh fruit — every type you could possibly imagine — was squeezed into juice by a team of twenty five-fruit crushers.

Very soon, Ria was bored. All the guests were busy guzzling their way through the mountains of delicious food, and slurping the fresh fruit juices. They were enjoying the party, and were not really interested in the young Princess. She really couldn't think of anything to say to them.

King Aman waited patiently, and when his guests had eaten and drunk all they could, he stood up to make a speech: "My friends, I have invited you to this party so we can have fun together. I want you to eat as much as you can, talk and laugh and enjoy yourselves. I also want to talk to you about my daughter, the very adorable Princess Ria. You know she is the light of my life, and I will do anything at all to make her happy. She is now sixteen years old. It is time to find her a husband, my friends, and I need your help . . ."

As the King talked on, everyone listened intently. Except for Princess Ria, who by now was very bored indeed. She slipped away from the party. If she'd stopped to think, she would have known that this wasn't a very sensible thing to do. However, Ria didn't stop to think. Why would she? Usually she never made her own decisions. She had no idea that dangers might lurk out there in the dark garden.

She was so quick that no one noticed a thing. She tiptoed through the bushes and into the dark of the garden. It was very peaceful amongst the plants and flowers, and she sat down for a while. She noticed bats skimming the tops of the bushes. She saw owls swooping down to find food. She spotted insects hiding amongst the leaves. She heard the rustle of snakes in the undergrowth. But Ria wasn't scared. Not at all. This was the first time in sixteen years that she had ever been alone, and she loved it.

Suddenly she heard a voice whispering through the leaves: "Ria! Ria! Where are you?"

"I'm here," she replied. "But where are *you*? And who are you? I can't see you."

Ria looked around, and suddenly from out of nowhere, a very good-looking young man appeared. He was wearing the golden robe of a Prince, a turban, sparkling rings and in his hand he carried a gleaming silver dagger or *kris*. "I am the Prince of Dreams. Putera Impian is my name. I've been trying to talk to you all night," the handsome stranger said. "My palace is nearby, in the forest. We are neighbours! I came to ask you to marry me!"

"Well," replied Ria, "I don't really want to marry anyone. But I'll happily talk to you. It's funny that I haven't met you before if you live so close."

"My palace is just close by," said the Prince. "Come with me and I'll show you."

Even though Ria thought she should ask her father's permission, she was intrigued. The Prince held out his hand, and she took it. In a split second she found herself before the most magical palace, with 450 rooms and 1,000 diamond-paned windows. A tower soared towards the sky, almost touching the moon. Giant mango trees grew in the garden and the air was heavy with the perfume of jasmine and other exotic flowers.

Prince Impian and Princess Ria sat in the garden and talked under the moon. She was surprised to discover that he was very funny and entertaining. He told her stories and she told him about her life. He really seemed like the nicest prince, and Ria thought that perhaps she had found someone she could marry after all. They chatted and laughed and forgot all about the time, until Ria, feeling dozy and contented, fell fast asleep.

As she slept she had the strangest dream. She dreamt that a little girl made a bed of emerald green moss for her, which was soft and velvety. As she lay down on it, she had a peculiar feeling that she was changing into a flower. The mysterious little girl, dressed in the colours of the forest, was whispering to her: "You are the keeper of the forest now, Ria. We have made you our Queen. You will be the largest flower in the forest and we will feed you all the year round. You are now Ria, Queen of the Forest."

When Ria woke up, the sun was already shining brightly.

"Oh no!" she exclaimed. "Father will be so mad with me. He'll think I'm lost. And where is Prince Impian? Why haven't my servants come to take me home, I wonder?"

As she tried to stand up she realized that she couldn't see the magical palace of the night before. In fact, she was at the edge of the forest, but still in her father's garden. Not only that, but she was rooted firmly to the ground.

Poor Ria! Too late, she remembered the stories that her servants had told her about the spirits of the forest. It was said that these spirits captured people who were wandering or lost — and they were never found again. Ria realized she had been tricked by these spirits. She had been transformed into a huge flower. Her legs and feet were now roots, reaching deep into the soil. She was rooted forever to the spot.

As time passed, she got used to her new life. The trees and shrubs around her protected her from danger. She was fed and looked after. In fact her life was not so very different from before. The only thing that made her sad was that she couldn't talk to her father.

King Aman never found out what happened to his daughter. He was heartbroken. He had a statue of her built in his garden, near to where she had disappeared, and he visited it every day. Nearby grew a large and rather beautiful plant, called the Rafflesia, which can still be found in the jungles of Malaysia. She grows to about a metre across and weighs several kilos. She blooms only once every four years. Little did the King know that this was his beloved Ria, now Queen of the Forest, quietly watching him.

PRINCE·PARAMESWARA
AND·THE·NAMING·OF
·S·I·N·G·A·P·U·R·A·

About seven hundred years ago, there lived a Prince named Parameswara. One of his worst enemies was the Raja of Majapahit from Java. The Raja was a mighty warlord, and everyone was afraid of him. His tall figure with its broad physique was quite awesome. As he strutted around in his colourful robes, people would fall at his feet to honour him. The Raja had hundreds of warships and thousands of soldiers, and he wasn't afraid to put them all to work. He often sent his warships across the seas to fight. Sometimes it was to win new land. Other times it was just for sport. He really cared very little for the lives of his people.

But there was one man he cared strongly about, and that was Prince Parameswara. He cared about him because this was the one person who challenged him constantly, like a mosquito always on the attack. He wasn't exactly dangerous, but he was very annoying. The Raja was a tiny bit afraid that one day this Prince would rally enough supporters to steal his powerful position. He knew he had to watch him very carefully.

Now Parameswara was not terribly nice either. He thought nothing of playing sport with someone one day, and having them punished the next, if they did not allow him to win. He was extremely tired of being bullied by this Raja. In fact he would do anything to annoy the man because he enjoyed causing trouble. Knowing that the Raja was growing suspicious of him, he decided to throw him a real challenge. He asked his palace woodcarvers to make him a lion throne, and once it was completed, he sent a message to inform everyone that he was now the Lion King. This message was really meant for the Raja to tell him that Prince Parameswara was now more powerful than he.

42

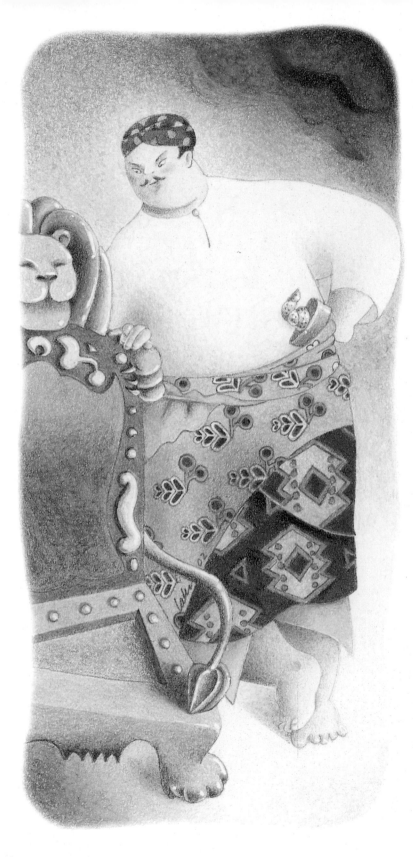

Of course, the very idea made the Raja really wild. Immediately he sent troops of soldiers and ships to drive Prince Parameswara out of the country.

When Parameswara heard the news, he didn't feel quite so brave any more. Once he had been told that forces were coming over land, and by sea, to drive him away, he panicked. He realized that this time he had gone too far. Because he was a complete coward, he did not stop and confront the Raja. He just hurried to the nearest available boat with some of his men, and left the country as fast as he could.

They sailed for two days and two nights, until they reached an island by the name of Temasek. White sandy beaches, fringed with coconut palms, stretched back from the water's edge. The scent of frangipani wafted towards them on the breeze. Behind the trees, lush, green jungle covered the land. Monkeys swung freely amongst the tree-tops, and large colourful crabs scuttled undisturbed across the sand.

43

The only people to be seen were two fishermen,
snoozing under a parasol on a boat nearby.
This was truly paradise.

"I know the King of this island,"
Parameswara told the crew. "He was a close
friend of my father's. I came here because
I know he'll welcome us with open
arms. He's known for his kindness
and hospitality."
He was quite right.
When the King heard of
their arrival, he rushed
out to meet them,
and greeted him and
his men like long
lost friends. He
took them to his
palace, prepared
a feast, and gave
Prince Parameswara
and his men palatial
rooms to sleep in.

"Don't worry!" the King said, when he heard Prince Parameswara's story. "You can hide out
here for as long as you like. The Raja will never dream of following you to this island. This is
a peaceful place. The only people here are fisher-people who have inhabited the island for
centuries. They are very calm and settled. You won't find any trouble here."

But Prince Parameswara had other plans. Remember, he wasn't such a nice person either. He had already caused trouble, threatened a ruler, and had to flee his own country. The seed of another wicked idea had already planted itself in his mind.

"Listen, men!" he whispered to them during the feast. "This is our perfect chance. If we kill the King, we can rule this country ourselves. The people of Temasek are quiet fisher-people. They won't stop us. Think how powerful we could be. We won't just stay here, we'll rule the place!"

So during the night, that kind King who had opened his doors to them, was killed in his bed while he slept. His family was loaded onto a boat with some provisions, and pushed out to sea. The next morning, Parameswara announced to the people of Temasek that he was their new King.

"I hereby change the island's name from Temasek to Singapura, or Lion City, after my carved and painted lion throne," he announced.

Sadly for the islanders, Parameswara was not a good King. He really knew nothing about how to run a country. He definitely did not know how to look after the people, protect them and make sure they were happy. After a while the once quiet fishing villages began to be attacked by pirates.

As Parameswara did nothing to stop the attacks, word soon spread to other islands, and Singapura was invaded by other people. The island became a very unsafe and difficult place to live.

As a result of this sad situation, many of the fisher-folk took their families and boats, and set sail for safer lands. They could not see any future in Singapura — and they decided to try to start new lives elsewhere. The island fell into ruin.

As attackers continued to try their luck against this Lion King, Parameswara again panicked. Because he was both a tyrant and a coward, he ran away for a second time, leaving the island to its fate. He was never heard of again.

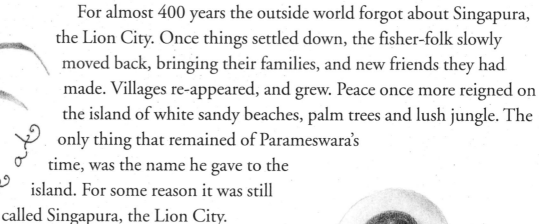

For almost 400 years the outside world forgot about Singapura, the Lion City. Once things settled down, the fisher-folk slowly moved back, bringing their families, and new friends they had made. Villages re-appeared, and grew. Peace once more reigned on the island of white sandy beaches, palm trees and lush jungle. The only thing that remained of Parameswara's time, was the name he gave to the island. For some reason it was still called Singapura, the Lion City.

Bigger ships from further away began to stop off at the island, on their way past. One day, a British man named Stamford Raffles landed, and decided that it would make a perfect port and trading post.

And the rest of the story, as anyone who lives in modern Singapore knows very well, is history!

46

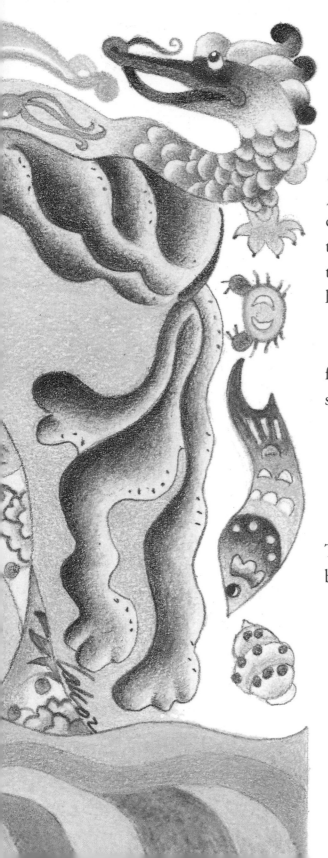

THE LUMINOUS PEARL

Long ago in the Eastern Sea lived a dragon king and his daughter Mai Li. She was a clever girl, and her father looked hard to find her an equally clever husband. But Mai Li didn't like the men who came to visit. Some were too tall, others too short, too fat, too thin, too rich, too vain, too serious . . . and so the list grew.

"So, what kind of man do you want?" asked her father.

"I don't need money, and I don't like people who are full of their own importance. I'd be more interested in someone who was poor, but honest and brave," came Mai Li's reply.

One day the King heard of a poor young man who lived by the bend in the river, at the foot of the tall mountain. He was known for his honesty and bravery. The King decided to put him to a test to see if he would be right for his daughter.

While the King was thinking up the test, this brave young man, Wei Jing, had a dream. He dreamt that a beautiful girl waited for him at the bend in the river. The dream was so real that he woke up with a start, and told his twin brother, Wei Ling, about it. Now Wei Ling was a nasty piece of work, and was always very jealous of his brother.

Wei Ling was even jealous that his brother had had such a dream. What if dreams came true? Then his brother would have a gorgeous girlfriend and Wei Ling would have no-one. In his most sarcastic voice, he said: "Dreaming again, are you? You know that dreams mean nothing. Just go back to sleep and forget it. It's rubbish!"

Wei Jing lay down again, and drifted back to sleep, but Wei Ling got dressed and crept off. You can guess where he was heading.

Wei Jing had the same dream again. There was the girl waiting for him by the bend in the river. Again it seemed so real that it woke him up. Although it was still dark, he noticed his brother had already gone out. He put on his clothes and rushed down to the bend in the river, only to find Wei Ling already there.

Before he could call out to him, something amazing happened. Silver moonbeams streaked across the sky. Glittering fireflies darted about, each one holding a shooting star. Standing on a rock in the middle of all this he saw Princess Mai Li, the girl from his dreams. Her gleaming black hair was so long that it trailed in the water like tendrils of seaweed.

Both brothers fell under her spell immediately. She also liked the look of both of them, because, being twins, they looked exactly alike.

"Which of you is honest and brave?" she called to them.

"I am!" they both replied at once.

"Then I'll have to give you a test. One of you must bring me a luminous pearl that shines in the night. The one who can manage that will be my husband. Right now, that pearl is in the keeping of the Dragon King of the Eastern Sea."

She gave each brother a magic scythe and said: "This will carve a passageway through the sea for you. You'll just have to manage the rest yourselves."

Wei Ling, afraid that Wei Jing might get to the pearl before him, rushed off at once, but Wei Jing stayed behind to get to know Mai Li better. The more he talked to her, the more he liked her. Eventually, after a long chat, he said goodbye and started out on his quest for the pearl.

He headed back to his hut first, to get some things for the journey. When he got there, he found that his brother had already cleared it of everything, including their only horse and every scrap of food. Wei Jing had no choice but to walk. For several days he struggled along on foot, without food, stopping only to pick fruit and to drink from the river.

Meanwhile, Wei Ling had arrived at a riverside village that had been hit by a massive flood. People everywhere were panicking. He asked a villager what was happening.

"Our village and crops have been devastated. We are starving. The only way to save the village is to go to the Dragon King and borrow his Golden Dipper," the villager told him.

"Just for you I will go there right now and pick it up, if you lend me a boat," said the sneaky Wei Ling, for we all know he was going there anyway.

The villagers were terribly grateful to him, and lent him a small boat to help him on his journey. So Wei Ling headed off in the boat across the swollen river, towards the Dragon King of the Eastern Sea.

Wei Jing arrived soon after this, and stopped to help the villagers, despite being very tired and hungry. He heard them talking about a magical Golden Dipper that they said was the only thing that could save them.

"I'm heading that way myself," he told them, "I will try to fetch it for you."

The villagers were happy to find someone else so keen to help, and offered to lend him a boat too. However, he thought the people needed it more than he did.

"No, thank you," he said politely, "I am strong enough to swim," and he dived straight into the river.

Swimming fast, Wei Jing crossed the choppy water, and after a while, he arrived at the edge of the rough and stormy Eastern Sea. The winds howled, the rain poured down and the waves were frighteningly high. At the water's edge was a small figure —crouched down and very scared. It was Wei Ling. He had been there for some time, but was too afraid to go near the water.

Not stopping to think, Wei Jing hurled himself into the waves, waving the magic scythe from side to side. The water immediately moved back, clearing a space for them to walk through. Wei Ling followed meekly behind without a word.

The Dragon King's palace was a vast cave. Green seaweeds were draped across the doorways. The entrance was studded with shells of different designs. Pearls were embedded in the massive main door, made from a giant clam shell. At the gate of the Dragon King's golden palace stood the King himself. Of course, the brothers had no idea that this was Mai Li's father.

"I am so very pleased to see you. I have been expecting you for some time. Please follow me to my treasure house," he smiled.

This turned out to be a small cave filled to bursting with riches. There were gems, jewels and glittering treasure chests. Some pieces were natural ones from the ocean bed. Others were beautiful objects salvaged from ships that had sunk in storms.

"You may look at everything, but can only take one item each," warned the King.

Wei Ling looked around greedily. Seeing a basket full of pearls, he picked out the biggest one with the most dazzling light. Whichever way you turned it, it shone like a mirror. Once he had the pearl, his greedy eyes could not tear themselves away from the other jewels in the room. Sparkling sapphires and dazzling diamonds seemed to beckon to him. He tried to steal a handful, but the guard was watching, and hurried him out.

Wei Jing also spotted the luminous pearls, but nobly remembered his promise to the villagers. In the middle of all the gems was the Golden Dipper, so he chose that. By the time he came outside, his brother had already gone without waiting. The Dragon King felt sorry for him, and personally escorted him to the border of his underwater kingdom.

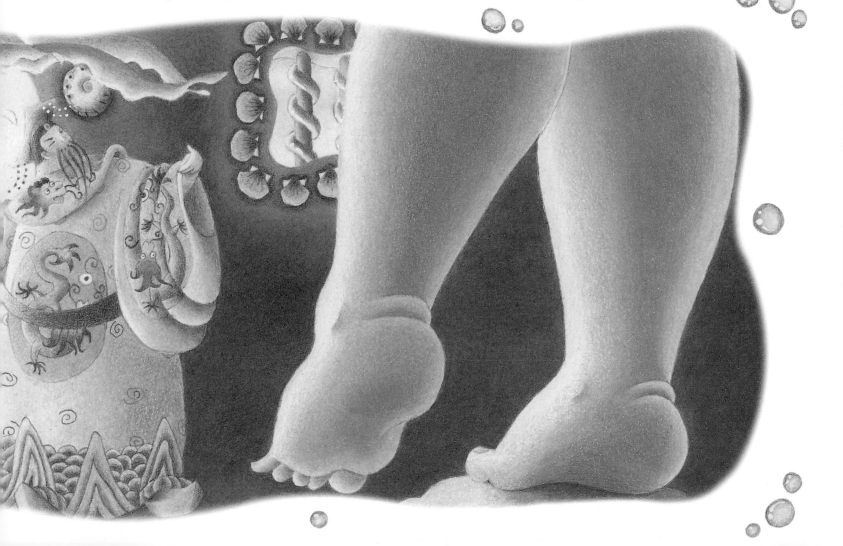

Of course, Wei Ling reached the flooded village first. A crowd of happy, eager faces rushed to greet him. "Did you bring the Golden Dipper?" asked the hopeful villagers.

"The Dragon King was mean and refused to lend it to me," lied Wei Ling, and before they could ask him anything else, he mounted his horse and galloped off, leaving the villagers sad and disappointed.

Soon after, Wei Jing arrived. He immediately brought out the Golden Dipper and began to scoop water. At once the flood waters moved back, revealing a huge oyster sitting on the riverbed. Inside the oyster was a large black pearl.

"This village hasn't seen an oyster like that for a hundred years," cried the villagers. "It's an omen. Give him the pearl as his reward."

Wei Jing was delighted. Although this black pearl was not what the Princess had asked for, it was still beautiful, and he was grateful to the villagers. He thanked them for their kindness, and took off as fast as he could to find Princess Mai Li.

Just as his brother arrived at the Princess's side, he caught up with him, and they both presented their pearls to her together.

"Thank you," she said, "We'll keep them until nightfall. Then we can see how they shine, and we'll know if they're genuine."

The brothers waited impatiently for the sun to go down. They busied themselves fishing, and resting, until evening fell. Looking very confident, Wei Ling sat by Mai Li when she took out his gorgeous, luminous pearl. But mysteriously the glow had gone, and it was now dull and lifeless. He snatched it from her, shook it furiously, polished it with his sleeve and breathed on it hard. None of this made any difference.

Wei Jing's pearl, however, dazzled like a million stars. It was so bright that Wei Ling had to close his eyes against its brilliance. By the time he opened them again, he found himself sitting all alone. Mai Li and Wei Jing had disappeared from sight. They were soon to be married and, like all fairytale couples, lived happily ever after.

VANISHED!

Long ago, when Singapore had just a few people living along its shores, a village or *kampung* grew in a shady spot, near to a large area of rainforest. The people who came to live here were Malays (from Malaya), and Javanese (from Indonesia). There were so many trees in the area, that even at midday the village remained quite dark. Because the village was shaded by the trees, many ghostly shadows formed, especially at sunset. The shadows were spooky, and frightened all but the most stubborn of children.

The newly arrived villagers were very superstitious, and felt sure that the forest was evil. Each family believed in something different — ancestral ghosts, wild animals, spirits that appeared in different forms and so on. There were lots of stories about people who vanished if they went into the forest. The village elder sternly warned the parents to tell their children not to play there.

"If you do, you will be munched by monsters," reminded one mother.

"Consumed by cruel creatures," muttered another.

"Stolen by spirits," came yet another.

Their warnings were very frightening, but mostly the children were far too afraid to venture into the forest anyway. Furthermore, they had plenty of other things to do. Early each morning they had their family chores to help with. The older ones had to fetch water from the village well, look after the younger children and feed the livestock. During the day when it was much too hot to run about, they would play *congkak* (a traditional board game with marbles) and chequers. But in the evening when the sun began to set, that's when the real fun began. All the *kampung* children would gather to play spinning tops, to chat, tease the village dogs, and to run wild.

Amongst the children were two mischievous boys named Din and Mahmud. They had been born within a day of each other, lived close to each other and had hardly spent a moment apart as they grew up. They weren't exactly naughty, but they were often in trouble, for they were very inquisitive children. If they were told not to do something, you could be sure they would try it anyway, just to see what happened. Din had fallen out of more trees than you can count. Mahmud's speciality was collecting insects and leaving them around for his nervous mother to find. Both of them had several younger brothers and sisters, which meant that their parents had very little time to spend following Din and Mahmud around. Amazingly, up until this day, they had never, ever broken the rule about going into the forbidden forest.

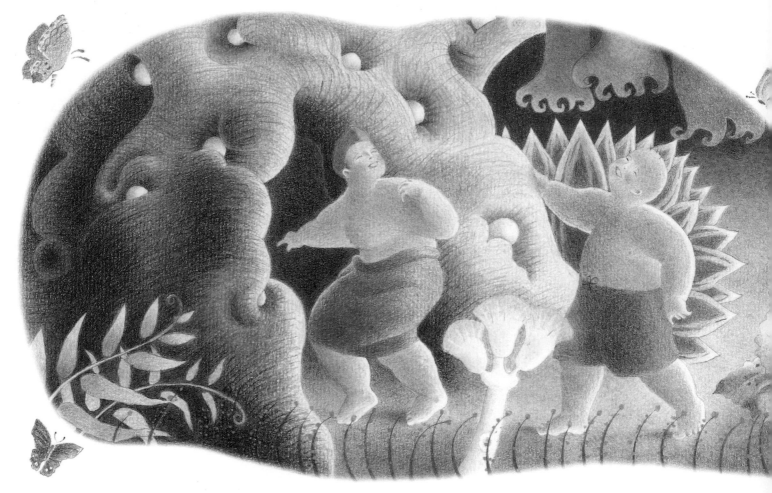

That evening as the children of the village played one of their favourite games of hide-and-seek near the forest, Din and Mahmud made a plan to trick everyone.

"This game is way too easy now," said Mahmud. "Let's make it harder for everyone. Let's hide in the forbidden forest. We needn't go too far in — just a little way will be fine. We're not really breaking the rule then."

"Good idea! No-one will find us there!" exclaimed Din without hesitating. "They'll never dream we would dare go inside! We'll be able to jump out and scare them all!"

So they sneaked off down the muddy track that led into the trees. As they drew near to the forest, they began to shiver. It was much cooler in the shade, and the air felt almost chilly. The silence of the forest and the quivering of the leaves gave them a ghostly feeling.

"M-m-maybe we shouldn't have come here," mumbled Mahmud, nervously.

"It's only for a moment," laughed Din. "There's nothing scary here. Just trees, that's all."

The game of hide-and-seek ended at sunset, but the other village children could not find Din and Mahmud anywhere. They searched everywhere. They called, and shouted, and screamed their names, but the boys seemed to have completely vanished.

Their younger brothers and sisters began to cry, not used to their big brothers leaving them behind like this. By now it was getting quite dark. The children grew frightened and ran to tell their parents.

"We were all playing hide-and-seek," they panted, "Din and Mahmud were winning because we looked everywhere but couldn't find them. Now it's getting dark and we want to give up, but they won't come out from their hiding places."

Din and Mahmud's worried parents ran straight out, calling their names, and hunting everywhere frantically trying to find them. A whisper went around that perhaps the forest spirits had snatched the boys, but no-one wanted to believe that. Every person in the village above the age of thirteen turned out to help in the search. They searched and called and called and searched, all that night and the next day. They looked up trees, inside water barrels, and under huts. Yet the boys could not be found. The villagers were now even more positive that something evil lived in the forest. Something that perhaps liked to trap human beings.

Had Din and Mahmud been eaten up by tigers? Or did something spooky really live in that forest? We will never know. After this, nobody wanted to go near the rainforest. If the villagers needed to gather firewood or herbs, they would go in groups, never with a child, and they certainly didn't venture too far inside.

What we do know is that the Javanese villagers named the village Cholang. The name is made from two Javanese words, *ucol*, which means to be released, and *hilang*, which means to disappear. The two words together warned that if anyone were to be let go into the jungle, they would vanish.

Many years later Cholang village and the rainforest were completely cleared and made ready for new buildings and new roads. Re-named the Watten Estate, the area changed completely and became a bright and friendly place to live. Since then, no-one has vanished in that area, and the story of Cholang has become a legend.

RAMANUJAN
AND THE
MIXED·UP WASHING

I t happened on a Tuesday. Ramanujan woke with a start, and as his mind began to clear from the jumble of dreams, he felt a niggle of excitement tucked away inside. The kind of feeling you get when you know something important is about to happen but you can't quite remember what it is. What could be happening today? He shook himself awake, and then remembered. Of course! Today he had been asked to do a very special job. He leapt to his feet, and in the dark he hastily began to get ready.

Rama was the youngest of the washer-men, or *dhobies*, who earned a living by collecting clothes from house to house, and washing them in the brown froth of the Singapore River. He was not quite sixteen, and until recently had worked alongside his father. Sadly his father had died, leaving Rama's mother to bring up five children alone. As the eldest son, it was now Rama's job to care for his family.

Rama had never been to school. Like many of the other *dhobies*, he could not read or write. He earned money by helping his Uncle Ganesan with his washing business. He learned how to collect the laundry from the big houses. How to behave while he was there. Who to speak to and who not to. How to listen carefully for instructions. How to watch the river for the tides. How to use the rocks for beating the dirt out, and how to spread the fabrics out on the flat ground to dry.

Last of all, he learnt the skill of sorting and folding the dry washing into bundles to be returned to the houses. This was probably the most difficult task. Because they could not read or write, the *dhobies* had invented their own methods of marking the washing piles so they never got muddled up. One mistake in this could lose a *dhoby* his job.

Rama was tall, strong and confident. Smooth dark hair swept low over his forehead, and when he smiled a flash of bright white teeth lit up his cheeky face. This Tuesday morning his smile was even wider than usual as he stepped onto the street. Yesterday Uncle Ganesan had given him an extra-special job to do. One to manage all by himself.

"Boy, I have too many collections tomorrow already," Uncle Ganesan told him. "The old amah from the corner house has asked me to take on their washing, and the washing of their neighbour Madam Fu. Their regular *dhoby* hasn't turned up for two weeks and she needs this doing urgently. She told me if I do this first job well she will give all the work to me. This is a big chance Rama, for you know which family she works for, don't you?"

Rama shook his head. He had no idea who these people were.

"The house is the big, fancy white one, with a white verandah and the huge garden with a banyan tree," his uncle explained. "It is called the house of Wong. A rich and distinguished Chinese family live there, and Mrs Li is the servant in charge. Next door is another Chinese family, the house of Fu it is called. This family also have washing to be done.

"These are very important jobs, Rama, and I am going to trust them to you. If you do them well, you won't have to work for me any longer. Take these jobs as your own. Remember all the things you have learned from your father and from me, because it's time now for you to work alone and earn some money to feed that family of yours."

Uncle Ganesan grabbed Rama's hand excitedly and began to shake it up and down. "But remember the golden rule Rama — don't mix up the laundry! Mrs Li will expect back the exact pieces she gave you and not one piece more or less. A mistake like that will lose you the job. Be careful! But of course you will, I don't have to tell you things like that," he beamed.

Rama was both proud and delighted. He hugged his Uncle and danced around the room clapping his hands in delight. Here was his chance to branch out on his own. His chance to take care of his family.

"Of course I can manage. I'll really make you proud of me, Uncle," he gasped. "How many times have I helped you with the same kind of problem? I'll be fine, don't worry. Thank you so much!"

He was so excited!

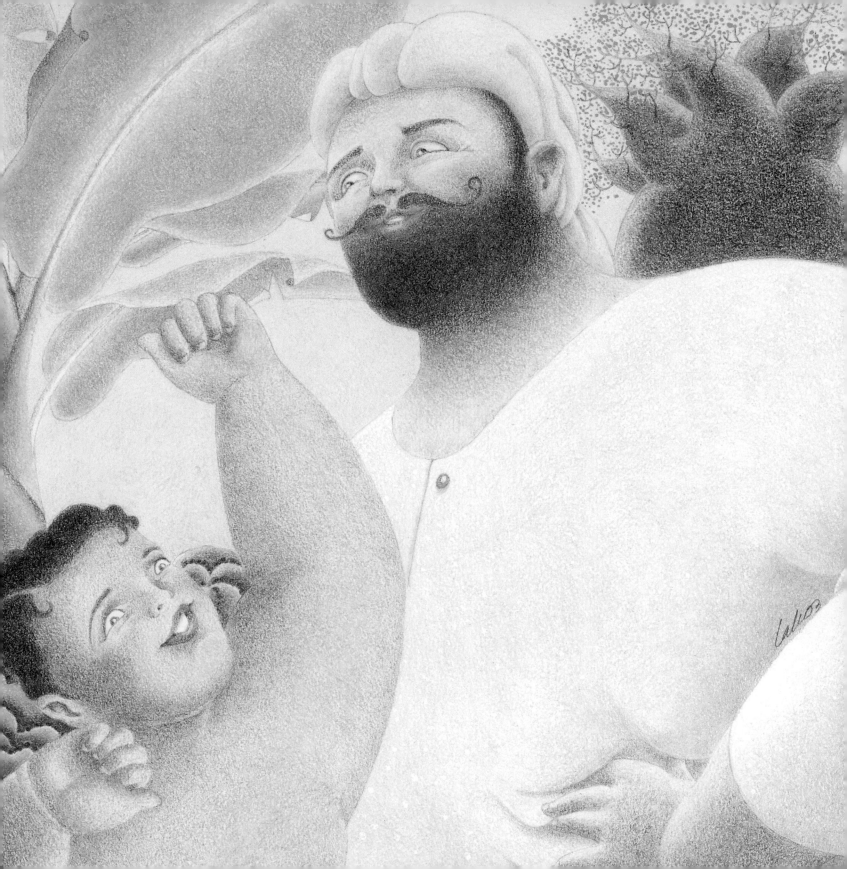

So it was on this particular Tuesday morning he strode out confidently towards the house of Mrs Li. It was a perfect morning. The sun rose brightly in a crystal-clear blue sky. What could possibly go wrong?

Wearing his whitest *lungi* (a type of Indian sarong), a piece of soft cotton cloth tied around his head, and clean but very faded and well-mended shirt, Rama marched proudly down the road that led towards the river. The street was already buzzing with life as the tradesmen plied their early morning trade. The *roti-wallah*, carrying freshly baked bread in a basket on his head, swayed past with a wave. *Dudh-wallahs*, milking mournful cows with twitching tails, sold fresh milk by the cupful from the road-side. A large straw basket bursting with pineapple skins stood to one side. The skinny-looking cows were fed on these once a day to make their milk even creamier. The garland-makers were already up and weaving their flower necklaces in the shophouse entrances, while the goldsmiths and sari-sellers inside, were getting their glittering goods ready to open for business.

Rama turned the corner, passing Bencoolen Street jail. Here the rickshaw-drivers washed their rickshaws at the road-side water tap near the prison building. Some chatted and played cards while they waited for a customer. Conical hats tied on with string, hung down their backs. Wearing dark shorts, short jackets and all with bare feet, they looked like boys waiting for the school doors to open.

Ah Chan's hawker stall was doing a brisk trade as usual, selling hot tea and coffee. Whistling cheerfully, Rama stopped to buy a cup of coffee from him, as he and his uncle did every morning.

"Morning, Boy! Where is Uncle?" wheezed the old coffee-hawker, as he poured the scalding coffee from a battered metal pot.

"Uncle is busy today. I'm working alone," replied Rama, hastily swigging down the steaming, sweet milky concoction.

"Good, good boy!" nodded Ah Chan. Rama, smiled and handed him a few cents.

He carried on his way down the road until he arrived at the gate of a large white bungalow. There was the verandah, and across a beautiful garden, the banyan tree. This must be the place! Heart thumping loudly deep inside him, Rama pushed the gate open and made his way to the back door. He knocked, and waited nervously.

An old Chinese lady opened the door, dressed in black. She looked him up and down for a second and then turned and shouted to someone inside.

"Wei Wei-ah! Bring washing quick quick! *Dhoby's* waiting. Hurry-lah!"

This must be Mrs Li, thought Rama. A girl appeared from nowhere staggering under the weight of two huge bundles. She dropped them at Rama's feet and disappeared inside.

Mrs Li spoke again. "Two washing. One this. One that." She pointed to her house and the house next door as she said the words, so there would be no mistake. "Back here 5 o'clock, boy. Understand? Yes or no?"

"Yes, 5 o'clock," Rama replied.

He bowed his head towards Mrs Li, picked up the bundles, threw them across his shoulder and made his way back to the road. So far, so good.

Now Rama headed for the river. Some of the other *dhobi-wallahs* were already there, standing in the river and slamming their washing against the rocks as they scrubbed and beat the dirt out. Rama found himself a space at the water's edge and opened up his bundles of washing.

Each bundle had table linen, children's clothes, handkerchiefs, napkins and other bits and pieces in. He arranged them on the bank, and with a stick he started to make squiggly marks in the dirt beside them. This was the way of many *dhobies*. To separate their washing they each had a kind of code to mark out which piece belonged to whom. Some scratched their codes onto the rock, or on a stick, and some etched it into the mud. Rama was in a hurry, so this is what he did now. He meticulously separated the two sets of washing, and made his list in the mud of how many pieces in which pile, and what they were.

He was very, very careful indeed.

The river was often brown and muddy, and washing things clean in it was no easy task. However, Rama scrubbed and rinsed, rubbed and rinsed, singing softly to himself as he did so. He was so absorbed in his task that he didn't notice the sky darken and the rain clouds rapidly blowing overhead. It wasn't until the first enormous drop of rain hit him squarely on the forehead and slithered down his nose that he looked up. As huge angry purple clouds gathered quickly overhead, a thunderclap split the sky in two and in no time at all the rain was falling down in torrents.

"No," yelled Rama, leaping out of the river, "NOOOOOO!" He grabbed at the piles of washing and ran for the shelter of the nearest tree. The other *dhobies* had already collected their things and were patiently sheltering and waiting for the rain to stop.

Rama squatted down by his pile of soggy washing and rocked backwards and forwards on his heels. He wasn't upset because it was raining. He was upset because in his rush to gather up the washing, he had carelessly thrown all of it together in one big muddy heap. Now it was all mixed up. He worried about what to do. No good asking the other washermen, they would only laugh and make fun of such a stupid mistake.

After a while the dark clouds passed, and the rain stopped as swiftly as it had started. Steam rose from the damp ground as the hot sun shone down once more. Rama spread the muddy, wet clothes out and stared at them miserably, trying very hard to remember where each piece had come from.

He felt a tap on his shoulder. "Rama, can I help you, boy?" It was Uncle Ganesan.

Rama shrugged his shoulders miserably and said: "I don't know, Uncle. I just can't remember how they were before the rain. I just panicked and ran. I made my list in the mud, and the rain has washed it all away. I'm so sorry to let you down. How could I be so stupid?"

"I'm here to help, boy," replied his Uncle, kindly. "We all do this once. Believe me, you won't make the same mistake twice! Now, let's help you sort this out as best we can. Think boy, think. Rack your brains. Tell me what you remember."

Together they tackled the problem. Not all of Rama's marks had been washed away by the rain, and he gradually remembered which belonged to who. With Uncle Ganesan calmly taking charge, piece by piece they sorted out two piles of laundry once again.

"Good. Now you must wash again Rama, but this time don't make your marks on the mud. Use something that won't get washed away — the clever ones use this." Fishing a drifting piece of bamboo from the fast flowing river, he pushed it into Rama's hands.

Now Rama remembered! Some of the other *dhobies* scratched their markings onto a stick with a knife and carried it around tucked into their *lungi*. Of course! That way it wouldn't get washed away in the rain. For each bundle of new laundry they used a new stick. Simple! Rama felt ashamed of himself for making such a stupid mistake. He began to scrub the washing clean all over again, and this time he didn't muddle it up. After that he dried it flat in the baking sunshine on the riverbank.

By 5 o'clock two bundles of sparklingly clean, neatly-folded washing were delivered back to Mrs Li's door.

"Wei Wei-ah!" he heard her shout. The girl appeared once more, took the washing inside, untied the bundles and examined the linen carefully, Rama held his breath.

Had he made a mistake? Had he muddled something?

Mrs Li was standing by with her hands on her hips, looking very serious. The girl nodded to her.

"OK boy!" said Mrs Li in a stern voice. "You come again next Tuesday morning, 6 o'clock. OK?" With a curt nod of her head, she handed him some money, and closed the door.

Yes! He'd done it! She had asked him to come back! Rama walked calmly back down the path to the road, but when he reached the corner, out of sight of the house, he leapt as high as he could in the air, and then began to run. He flew home as fast as he could to give his mother his hard-earned money.

That was the start of Rama's laundry business. He never forgot the lesson of the muddled washing, and if you had been able to visit Rama a few years later, you would have found a cheery young man with his own shop front, and a fine sign outside that read: 'Ramanujan — finest laundry in town.'

THE · PIRATES OF · RIAU

Around a hundred years ago, fearsome pirates were often found sailing in the waters around Singapore. The most famous — and most feared — pirate at this time was Chief Black Buffalo, or Kerbau Hitam. He was dark and ferocious looking, but not as you might be thinking with a wooden leg and an eye patch. Kerbau Hitam wore just a cloth around his middle, with a sharp knife tucked into it, and a bandanna around his head to keep the sweat out of his eyes.

His men were dressed the same way. Their feet were also bare, so they moved stealthily and silently. Kerbau Hitam had fearsome black eyebrows that met in the middle of his forehead, and a permanent scowl. He would slay a dozen men, dust off his hands, and then sit down to breakfast without a thought. His face had such a ferocious look on it that many people fled without a battle. His band of pirates were as fierce and vicious as he.

74

Now, Kerbau Hitam and his gang were planning a new attack. They had heard a rumour that the Raja of Riau's daughter was planning to get married. A royal wedding meant that plenty of gold and jewels would be around for easy picking. They just had to figure out how to get their hands on the loot — and do it quickly and stealthily.

"We all know that the Raja of Riau will be very wary," said Kerbau Hitam to his men. "He'll suspect everyone and everything. He'll do everything in his power to protect the island against any form of attack, which makes this mission very dangerous, but it'll be fun! If we're not very careful, he'll spot us immediately and set his army onto us."

"I have a plan," he continued. "We will disguise ourselves as traders from Johore, bringing goods for the wedding."
He finished with a harsh laugh: "The rest . . . you can guess!"
The men rubbed their hands together with excitement. They continued to discuss how the rest of the plan would work well into the night.

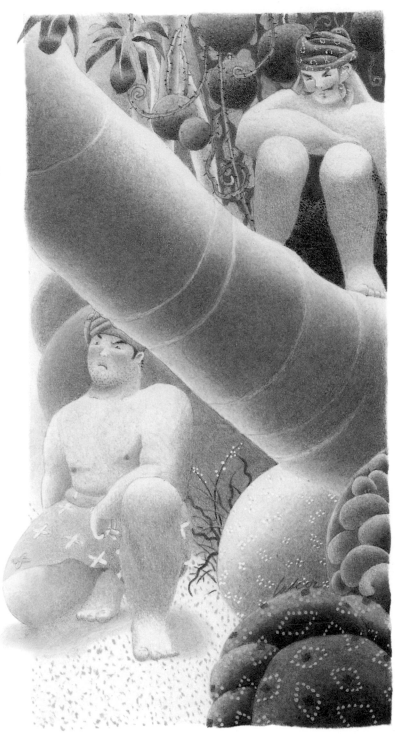

Preparing crates of goods to carry onto the island to show they were traders took some time, but when all the preparations were complete, they set sail for the Riau islands on their heavily disguised pirate junk.

When they arrived, and landed at the shore, the Raja's guards came down to their boat to meet them.

"In the name of the Raja, before you set foot on this land, who are you?" enquired the first guard.

"Traders from Johore, selling fabric and lace," Kerbau Hitam replied confidently. "The Raja is expecting us."

The Raja's daughter, Normah, was at that moment planning her wedding gown with a team of tailors. The whole island knew about this, and that she was waiting for a delivery of fabric from the mainland. The Raja's soldiers thought this must be a batch of fabric arriving for the princess's dress, and they did not suspect a thing.

"Welcome! Bring your goods ashore," said the guard.

Within minutes he wished he had never got up that morning. The pirates grabbed him, tied him up and overpowered the rest of his shore patrol. The pirates then sauntered up to the Raja's palace and calmly walked in the front door.

As soon as they entered the palace, the Raja came out to greet them. Four pirates immediately surrounded him, grabbed him and bound his feet and hands together. The whole job had so far taken no more than ten minutes. Kerbau Hitam stepped forward, his silver knife glinting in his hand, and the famous scowl on his face.

"People of the palace, DON'T make the mistake of trying to help your Raja. The island is now under our control. If any of you try to stop us, we will kill the Raja immediately, in front of your eyes." He turned to his men and said: "Tie up anyone you find. We'll deal with them later."

And so, the helpless Raja was taken prisoner in his own palace, while his daughter still sat innocently planning her wedding in her room, not yet knowing that pirates surrounded her.

Suddenly the door to her room was flung open, and in strode the most terrifying man she had ever seen. Behind him, tightly bound, her father shuffled along, being pushed from behind by another vicious-looking man. Kerbau Hitam took one look at the Princess and decided she would do just fine as a pirate bride.

"I'll marry your daughter if you like, old man," chuckled the pirate.

"Never," declared the Raja, "You'll have to kill me first."

Normah screamed when she heard this, but the pirate only laughed harder. "Lock her up. She'll soon change her tune when she's tired and hungry."

Down by the seaside, Normah's fiancée, Rahim, had returned from a hunting trip just in time to see the pirates arrive. Hidden in some nearby trees, he had watched everything helplessly. Without being seen, he jumped aboard a small boat, and sailed to Singapore to get help. Within a day he landed at Tanjong Rhu and told the fishermen gathered on the shore his terrible tale. They took him immediately to their leader or *temenggong*.

The *temenggong* was horrified. He had heard that Kerbau Hitam's men were plundering all the islands in the area. He agreed to help stop the pirates, and asked for support from a Chinese headman.

That night the headman called a meeting with twenty of his most trustworthy men, to discuss what they could do. All night they talked and argued and drew maps, and by the time the sun came up the next morning they had hatched a plan.

Before dawn, a fine Chinese junk set sail for Riau. Aboard were the *temenggong* and Rahim, disguised as Chinese labourers, together with the Chinese headman and his twenty men. When they arrived at the very shore that Rahim had left the previous day, it was teeming with pirates. Rahim rowed alone to shore in a small boat to make contact.

"Good evening, sirs. Can I speak to your Raja?" asked Rahim, approaching the most feisty-looking character he could see.

"I am the Raja here, what is your business?" grunted Kerbau Hitam.

"We're heading for Singapore, but we have a dead man on board our junk who needs burying immediately. If you allow us to stop and bury him, we can offer you a reward."

"A reward eh? And what exactly are you willing to pay?" asked Kerbau Hitam, arms behind his back and puffing out his chest with sudden interest.

"We're carrying a cargo of gold. We're willing to pay you a substantial amount in gold bars if you'll let us land for a short time."

"Agreed," replied Kerbau Hitam, "but you must bring your whole crew with you. My men will guard your boat and your gold."

So Rahim returned to the junk, and rowed back to shore carrying the *temenggong*, the coffin and only seven men. The rest, of course, were still in hiding on the junk.

They picked up the coffin and began carrying it towards the trees that grew thickly above the tide-level.

"Stop! Wait! Are you armed?"

"Of course not," replied Rahim calmly. "We are only here to bury a dead man. By all means, search us."

The pirates searched them, but of course, found nothing. Not wanting to disturb the dead body, they dared not open the coffin to check it.

Meanwhile, Kerbau Hitam and his men rowed out to the junk. Their plan, as you've probably guessed, was to rob the junk, while the crew on land were burying their dead.

"Seize him," came a bloodcurdling cry, and the thirteen sailors hiding on board leapt out, seized the pirates, bound their feet and hands, and locked them up in the twinkling of an eye.

At the same time, back among the trees, the Chinese sailors opened the coffin and took out the weapons that were hidden inside. Quickly they ran to the Raja's house, captured the other pirates and freed the Raja, Normah and the villagers held there.

Rahim and Normah decided to get married as soon as possible. The Raja thanked everyone, especially the *temenggong* from Singapore and his men. He invited them all to come back for the wedding feast.

Kerbau Hitam and his pirate gang were hanged for piracy. They were not, however, the last pirates to plague Singapore waters. The seas around the island provided the perfect short-cut for many cargo boats, giving pirates plenty of chances to add to their booty. The small islands off-shore gave them perfect places to lie low.

Some of Singapore's islands may still have pirate treasure buried on them somewhere. Dig deep enough and you may find it.

THE TWO WIDOWS

Far away among the rice fields there once lived two widows named Wan Malini and Wan Empok. They had lived together since their husbands had died. They were good women, who had spent their lives planting the rice crop or *padi* on the slopes of one of Singapore's hills, Bukit Si-Guntang.

They were kind to the children of the village, making special things for them when it was festival time. If anyone came to their door asking for something, Wan Malini and Wan Empok never turned them away empty-handed, even though they had very little themselves.

Seven days a week they worked the fields. If their rice crop failed, they would be left with nothing. Tending the crops then, was their life. In the evenings they did the household chores and looked after their animals.

Going to bed at sundown, and getting up at sunrise meant that there was never a moment of spare time. Day in and day out, the women worked extremely hard and never complained about their lot.

One dark and silent night came a thundering noise, so loud that it woke the women out of their deep sleep.

"What is that noise?" called out Wan Malini in a quavering voice.

"I think it must be elephants. Yes, that's what it is. Trumpeting elephants," replied Wan Empok.

"But if the elephants are trumpeting, that means they are also trampling. And if they're trampling, our *padi* will be destroyed," wailed Wan Malini.

She was quite right. If the elephants really *were* on the rampage, then their crops would be done for. The two women would have nothing left to eat or sell in the market and would certainly starve. They got dressed and rushed out of their house as fast as they could, only to see a bright light glowing on the far hill.

"Now I'm really scared. What can it be?" cried Wan Malini nervously. "Is the hill on fire?"

"No," said Wan Empok, sniffing hard. "If it were on fire we would be able to smell the burning."

"Could it be fire from a dragon's mouth, or a monster, or a glowing jewel?" asked Wan Malini, her imagination running riot.

They huddled in their doorway for a while and watched, and waited, and worried themselves silly. Only then, when they were worn out with worry, and propped up on each other, did they drop off to sleep.

When they woke up, stiff and sore, the sun was already shining. They stared hard at the hillside, which was gleaming and glittering gold in the sunlight.

Wan Malini, feeling braver after her sleep, said: "Let's climb the hill now and find out what was glowing in the night."

This time it was Wan Empok's turn to be more timid. "You're mad! We can't go alone, just us two women! We might need help. What if it's a vicious beast?"

"Oh come on! We can take a peek and run away if it's anything too scary," came her friend's reply.

Together they climbed the hill cautiously, stopping to peer into the distance from time to time, but they saw nothing except the glow, which got brighter as they drew nearer. To their astonishment they discovered that their rice *padi* was growing golden grains, with silver leaves and golden stems.

"Aiyee! So this is what we saw! But how did it happen?" said Wan Malini, whispering with disbelief.

They climbed higher, and to their amazement saw three elephants. Riding the elephants were three young men, looking like princes, wearing brightly coloured, jewel-studded turbans. They each wore a shimmering silk costume, decorated with silver filigree, with a cape that flowed down to their knees.

"Who are you and where are you from?" asked Wan Malini in her bravest voice.

"Are you magic? The sons of fairies or genies, perhaps?" asked Wan Empok.

The three men replied together: "We have come from Dika. Our father is the great Raja of Kalinga, like our grandfather before him. Our mother is the Princess of Dika. We inherited magical powers from them."

The two widows were mesmerised by the exciting story the men began to tell, but when they had finished Wan Malini was still suspicious. She folded her arms across her chest and spoke out: "This all sounds very splendid, but can you prove any of it? How do we know you're not a gang of cheats?"

The royal princes took turns to reply. "The turbans that we wear show our royalty."

"If you don't believe in our powers, look at your *padi* fields. We have heard about you, and the way you have dedicated your lives to growing excellent *padi*."

"We turned your *padi* into gold and silver for you, so you will never be poor again. From now on this hill will be a sacred place, and you will always grow golden rice grains."

Like most country people, Wan Malini and Wan Empok really believed in magic, and so they bowed before the royal princes. They even took them down the hillside to their house, and prepared a simple, but delicious, feast for them in their tiny kitchen. Once the princes had eaten, they rode away on their elephants and were never seen on Bukit Si-Guntang again. It was as if the whole thing had been a dream.

But from that day on the *padi* field of the two widows produced gold and silver for the rest of their lives. If you ever come close to Bukit Si-Guntang, look carefully. It doesn't matter if the weather is bright or dull, the mountain slopes shimmer like a precious metal.

THE MAGICAL PRINCESS

ong, long ago, deep in the misty rainforests of Malaysia, lived a princess. She was known as Putri Gunung Ledang, or the Princess of Mount Ophir (which is much easier to say, don't you think?).

Mount Ophir was a giant mountain that lay across the border separating the states of Melaka and Johor. The Princess of this mountain was a strange and magical girl, with such great powers that she could transform herself into thirty different people. She could be an old woman one moment, a beautiful young girl the next. She could switch from servant to child to queen without even taking a breath. Many men were fascinated at the thought of such an interesting girl. Someone like her would never be boring, would she? Several wanted to marry her, and countless others had tried already, but she refused them all.

A few suitors had given up when they saw how tricky the journey was to visit her, for the princess's palace was built on the very summit of Mount Ophir. The steep slopes leading up to it were covered with dense jungle. Many princes had already tried to reach the princess, but had failed. One or two were taken by tigers, known to roam the slopes by day. The people who lived by the mountain believed that the tigers might be the princess in one of her disguises.

Others just weren't fit enough to climb such a steep slope and gave up half way, huffing and puffing heavily. Still others took one look through their royal telescopes and did not even attempt to begin the trek.

It just so happened that the Sultan Mahmud Shah of Melaka was looking for an extraordinary girl to be his bride. His wife had died just a few months earlier, leaving him sad and lonely, with a baby son to care for. He had heard tales of this princess, and the stories fascinated him. He thought that she sounded enchanting, and he decided to see if she would be interested in him.

He also heard that the princess could be rather awkward. Not wanting to leave his son for any length of time, he asked his best friend, Hang Nadim, a favour.

"To save me some time, would you go up there first? Go and ask her if she would consider marrying me, the Sultan Mahmud Shah of Melaka. If she seems enthusiastic, I'll definitely go up there in person next week."

Hang Nadim prepared well for the trip, as he wanted to do his very best for his friend. With the help of the Sultan's advisors, he arranged for a team of horses. On the first horse he hung bags filled with glittering gold coins. On the second he placed bags overflowing with fine, flowing fabrics. The third carried baskets of gorgeous gem-stones, and in the fourth basket he placed succulent hand-made sweets cooked by the Sultan's own palace chefs.

With the horses laden down with these goodies, and six servants to help him, he set off on the journey to find the princess.

Hang Nadim, his horses and his six servants struggled through the tough terrain. They stopped to rest, half way. Suddenly, an old woman appeared in front of them. She was horribly ugly, with straggly black hair, a truly awesome nose, and eyebrows like furry tarantulas. She was leaning on a stick. She pointed the stick up the mountainside.

"I've been sent here to guide you," she croaked.

As she spoke, a pathway lit up in front of them. It glowed in the dark, showing the way to the top of the mountain. Hang Nadim wondered if this was the princess in one of her many disguises. But by the time he turned to take another look at her, she had already vanished.

The group struggled on, eager to get to the top in case the light went out. As they reached the palace, the main doors swung open. Dragging their weary bodies inside, they saw the princess. She was sitting on a throne draped with shimmering royal red velvet. Hang Nadim threw himself at her feet.

"Salaam, Princess!" he greeted her. "My name is Hang Nadim. My closest friend is Sultan Mahmud Shah of Melaka. He is a very busy man, but has heard so much about you that he thinks he wants to marry you. He has sent me here to meet you, and to see if you are interested in meeting him too. He has sent you all these gifts."

As Hang Nadim spoke, the servants brought the gifts and laid them in front of the princess. She stood with her arms folded and a very haughty expression on her face.

"The Sultan's gifts don't impress me," she said. "I've seen better things than this. And expensive presents certainly don't prove love. If he is so keen on me, he must complete three tasks. Listen hard because you will have to remember everything I tell you: First, he must build a bridge of solid gold between his kingdom and mine. Then I can visit him whenever I want. Second, he must bring me seven trays of mosquito hearts, because they are the most difficult things to catch, and they bite me all night long. Lastly, I want a cup of blood taken from his son's right hand. These tasks must all be done by a week from today. Then I will decide if he is worth marrying or not."

With that, the princess stood up and left the room. The exhausted men were shown to a side room where food and drink had been prepared, with enough beds for them all. They knew that early the next morning they would have to return to the Sultan with the Princess's extraordinary message.

The next day, before dawn, the servants and horses followed Hang Nadim back down the mountain to the Sultan's palace. Hang Nadim went straight to see his friend.

"Welcome back — and so soon!" said the Sultan. "And what's the news? When will she marry me?"

Hang Nadim told him of the princess's demand for a golden bridge. The Sultan clapped his hands in excitement.

"I knew she would ask for something interesting," he shouted, "Now, I must think carefully. Where will I get all this gold from?"

"The quickest way is to collect it from your people," suggested Hang Nadim. "They won't like it, of course, but if you tell them that it is for the Sultan's marriage, they might be more willing.

"But there's another task too. She wants seven trays of mosquito hearts."

The Sultan laughed. "She is playing games," he said. "That's easy. Anything else?"

"Well," Hang Nadim hesitated, not really wanting to tell him about the third task, "She wants a cup of blood taken from your son's right hand."

The Sultan's face fell. "What? That's too much to ask. It's madness. I'll complete the first two tasks and then I'll ask her again. She can't possibly be serious about that."

Without wasting any more time, the Sultan gave orders for all the soldiers in his army to tour the country, asking every family to hand over its gold, by order of the Sultan. He asked for the best zoologists to catch mosquitoes without squashing them, and remove their hearts.

The finest engineers and goldsmiths were brought to the Palace to design the bridge. As the gold rolled in, labourers worked day and night. Some smelted the gold, others laid the foundations, and others cleared a space through the jungle. For six days and six nights one thousand workers toiled non-stop, until at last the bridge was completed. Everyone agreed that it was beautiful. Not only that, but the princess would now be able to come and go across the bridge as often as she liked. The seven trays of mosquito hearts were ready and waiting. The only thing missing was the cup of blood.

The night before he was going to travel to meet the princess, the Sultan went into the room where his son was sleeping peacefully. He was just a baby, six months old. Taking a whole cup of blood from him would certainly kill him. The Sultan knew that he could never, ever do such a thing. No princess was worth that kind of sacrifice. As he sat with his head in his hands, a glowing light filled the room. A beautiful young woman stood in this light. As he watched, she changed into an old hag with spider-like eyebrows, then into a tiger, then back into a beautiful woman again.

She spoke. "I am the princess of Mount Ophir. I am happy that you can't kill your son for me. That shows you are a good man. But, it also means that you can't finish the tasks I set for you, so I won't marry you."

As she finished speaking she began to change again. She turned into thirty different women in quick succession, each one more beautiful than the last, until finally she vanished.

Sultan Mahmud breathed a sigh of relief. How could he have been so silly as to want to marry someone with such awesome powers? He shuddered at the thought. How could he ever trust anyone like that? She really was quite mad.

The story of the princess and her strange demands spread like wildfire. Since then, no prince dared to ask to marry her, and she spent the rest of her life alone. In fact, no-one really knows what happened to her after that. The gorgeous golden bridge was soon over-run by the same jungle that covers Mount Ophir. And the Sultan never remarried, and spent the rest of his life happily caring for his son.

Sources

Asean Tales and Legends, System's
　　　Readers by Catherine Siew,
　　　System Publishing House Pte Ltd,
　　　Singapore
Her Fathers' Kingdom and Other Tales,
　　　System's Readers by Sutimah Roowi,
　　　System Publishing House Pte Ltd,
　　　Singapore
Lion City, by Sutißah Roowi, System
　　　Publishing House Pte Ltd,
　　　Singapore
Tales from the Islands of Singapore, by Ron
　　　Chandran-Dudley, Landmark Books
　　　Pte Ltd
The Luminous Pearl: A Chinese Folk Tale,
　　　retold by Betty Lore, illustrated by
　　　Carol Inouye, Orchard Books,
　　　New York
Singapore: Pages of Our History, Tan Ee Sze,
　　　Pan Pacific Publications (S) Pte Ltd

Book design by Periplus Design Team
Editing by Kim Inglis

ABOUT TUTTLE:
"Books to Span the East and West"

Our core mission at Tuttle Publishing is to create books which bring people together one page at a time. Tuttle was founded in 1832 in the small New England town of Rutland, Vermont (USA). Our fundamental values remain as strong today as they were then—to publish best-in-class books informing the English-speaking world about the countries and peoples of Asia. The world has become a smaller place today and Asia's economic, cultural and political influence has expanded, yet the need for meaningful dialogue and information about this diverse region has never been greater. Since 1948, Tuttle has been a leader in publishing books on the cultures, arts, cuisines, languages and literatures of Asia. Our authors and photographers have won numerous awards and Tuttle has published thousands of books on subjects ranging from martial arts to paper crafts. We welcome you to explore the wealth of information available on Asia at **www.tuttlepublishing.com**.